THE MIGHTY LIONS & THE BIG MATCH

BY **TOM CHAPMAN**

ILLUSTRATED BY **CHRIS DICKASON**

WELBECK

The Mighty Lions & the Big Match is a reminder that children can often feel a lot of pressure in their social relationships, at school, in the arts and on the sports field, as highlighted in this book. Children are particularly sensitive to the messages that adults send to them, however well-intentioned, and can misinterpret any eagerness for them to succeed. This sports-themed book helps show that they can find support and hope in the future, even in the face of disappointment. And it also helps show adults that we can be driving forces to help children enjoy their activities and reduce any performance-related worries they might have. *The Mighty Lions & the Big Match* is a wonderfully appropriate book for children and adults to read and discuss together, especially for the sports fans among us!

Lauren Callaghan
Consultant Clinical Psychologist

Abel's team, the Mighty Lions, had made it to the final.
They were playing for the cup!

From the changing room, Abel saw the crowd gathering.

"There are a lot more fans than I expected, Drake," said Abel to his brother.

A shiver went through his fur.

"Now everyone, pay attention," said Coach. "Today we must beat the Tigers and win the cup!"

Abel looked at his teammates. Were they nervous like him?

"OK, Lions – game time!" Coach said.

The Mighty Lions walked out onto the pitch, to the roar of their parents and friends cheering from the sidelines.

"Come on, Lions!"

"Mighty Lions CAN do it!"

"You MUST win the cup!"

The Tigers looked much older and stronger than the Mighty Lions.

"What if we *don't* win the cup?"
Abel said. "What will Coach think?
What will Mum and Dad think?"

"No worries, bro,"
Drake replied. "We'll win."
Drake didn't seem
bothered at all, which
made Abel feel even
more nervous.

Was he the only one?

Abel was staring at the Tigers when, suddenly, the ref blew the whistle. The final began!

The Tigers started strong, attacking the goal with shot after shot.

"Tackle those Tigers! I can't do all the work!" Drake growled.

The Mighty Lions ran up and down the pitch, working as a team.
As the pressure grew, they started making mistakes.

Drake grew angry with his teammates.

But Drake was the Lions' goalkeeper,
and he saved the ball each time.

Another Tiger kicked the ball into the box.

Drake made the save!
"Phew!" Drake said.

But – oops – he passed the ball to a Tiger, who took his chance and scored!

The ref blew the whistle again, and the first half was over.

"What were you thinking?!" shouted Coach. "Why would you do that?!" shouted the crowd.

Drake wanted to run ... and hide.
Instead, he dragged his feet over to Abel.

"It's OK, bro," Abel said. But they both knew it might not be.

When the second half kicked off, the Mighty Lions stormed up the pitch.

Winnie took a shot at the goal ... but she missed.

"Better luck next time, Winnie," said Coach.

Winnie ran down the pitch again, with confidence.

This time, she scored!

The Mighty Lions all roared. They were back in the game!

Drake saved another shot, but then kicked the ball out of play.

"Come on, Drake. Pass it to one of *our* players next time," said Coach.

Drake turned red.

Time was quickly running out, and the Mighty Lions were getting tired.

Abel won back the ball and ran ... but was blocked on all sides by huge Tigers.

"Pass the ball, son!" roared Abel's dad.

Abel suddenly stopped and looked at his dad. *I can't do anything right,* he thought. Tears blurred his eyes, then –

OOF!

He was tackled by a Tiger.

Hooray! This was their chance to win, and with only a minute left in the game!

Coach nodded to Abel to take the penalty.

He stepped up with only a moment to think.

If I score this goal, we could win the cup! But if I miss, I will lose this for everyone.

Abel held his breath, stepped forward to kick and ...

HE MISSED!

The Tigers pounced.
"Let's finish this off!" they growled and bolted down the pitch.

Drake was no match for the
fierce attack. The ball soared
into the back of his net.

And the Mighty Lions ... well, they didn't feel so mighty.

"How did you miss that?" Coach asked Abel.
"Abel, we could have won the cup," said Winnie.

All Abel could do was shrug. He knew he had let everyone down.

"Why did you pass that ball to their striker, Drake?" asked Mum.

"And how did you miss that penalty, Abel?" asked Dad.

"There was so much pressure on us, Dad," Abel answered.

"It was like we had to win the cup for everyone watching," added Drake.

"I kept worrying that we could lose," said Abel. "And then we did. It made the game not fun to play."

"Wow," said Mum and
Dad. "We didn't realise."

They opened their arms
wide, and Abel and Drake
walked right into giant
hugs. They stayed there
for quite a while.

"We're sorry we put so much pressure on you to win," said Mum and Dad.

"But you played your best and that's all that matters," said Mum.

Abel and Drake hugged
their parents tighter.
The stress of the game
began to melt away.

"This was just one game among many you will play in your lives," added Dad. "You will win some, and you will lose some. You can decide to learn from your losses and turn them into wins."

"Either way, we love you – not the result of game."

Abel and Drake let out huge sighs. The young cubs realised that even though they had lost this match, it didn't make them failures.

"We'll come back next season, better than ever!" said Drake.

"Yes, we will! Because we're Mighty Lions!" cheered Abel.

To my amazing boys, everything they are and all they will become.
I will love you always, no matter what. If you can't be anything else,
be kind and courageous. – T.C.

An Upside Down Book

Published in 2021 by Welbeck Children's Books
An Imprint of Welbeck Children's Limited, part of Welbeck Publishing Group.
20 Mortimer Street London W1T 3JW

Copyright © Tom Chapman 2021
Illustration Copyright © Chris Dickason 2021

A CIP catalogue record for this book is available from the British Library.

ISBN 978-1-78956-244-6

Printed in Dubai

10 9 8 7 6 5 4 3 2 1